THIS WALKER BOOK BELONGS TO:

_____

_____

_____

_____

To Calla, two years hence
A.B.

For Caitlin
J.L.

First published 1998 by Walker Books Ltd
U/ Vauxhall Walk, London SE11 5HI

This edition published 1999

2 4 6 8 10 9 7 5 3 1

Text © 1998 Alison Boyle
Illustrations © 1998 Julie Lacome

This book has been typeset in Gill Sans Bold Educational.

Printed in Hong Kong

British Library Cataloguing in Publication Data
A catalogue record for this book is
available from the British Library.

ISBN 0-7445-6971-0

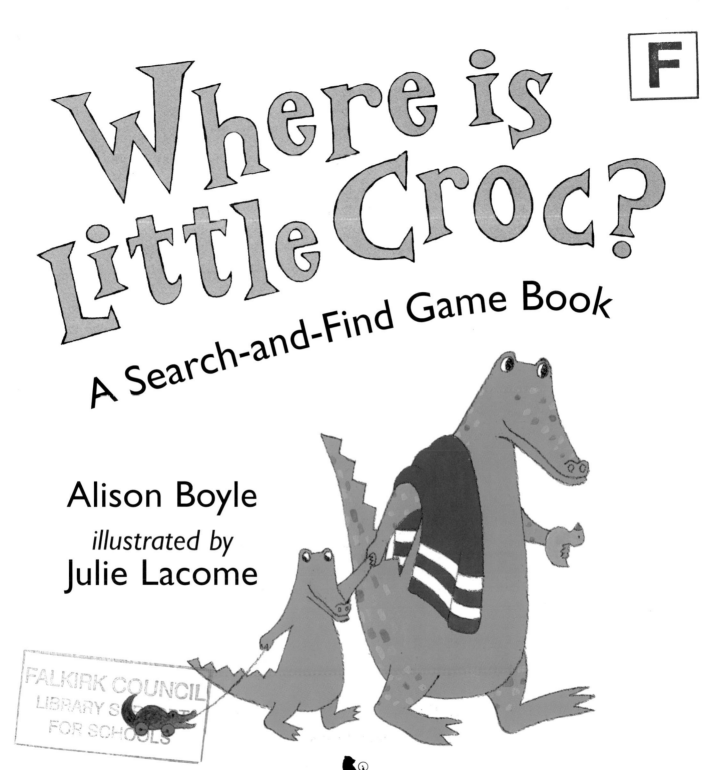

Where is Little Croc?

A Search-and-Find Game Book

Alison Boyle

illustrated by
Julie Lacome

WALKER BOOKS
AND SUBSIDIARIES
LONDON • BOSTON • SYDNEY

F

Mum was getting Little Croc's bath ready.

But Little Croc wasn't ready for his bath. He had a better idea.

Little Croc hid in the living room.

Where are you,
Little Croc?

Can you find Little Croc?
And can you find Muncher?

Little Croc hid in the kitchen.

Can you find Little Croc?
And can you find Swish?

Little Croc hid in the playroom.

Can you find Little Croc?
And can you find Spiky?

Little Croc hid on the landing.

Can you find Little Croc?
And can you find Grin?

Little Croc hid in the bedroom.

Where are you, Little Croc?

Can you find Little Croc?
And can you find Monster?

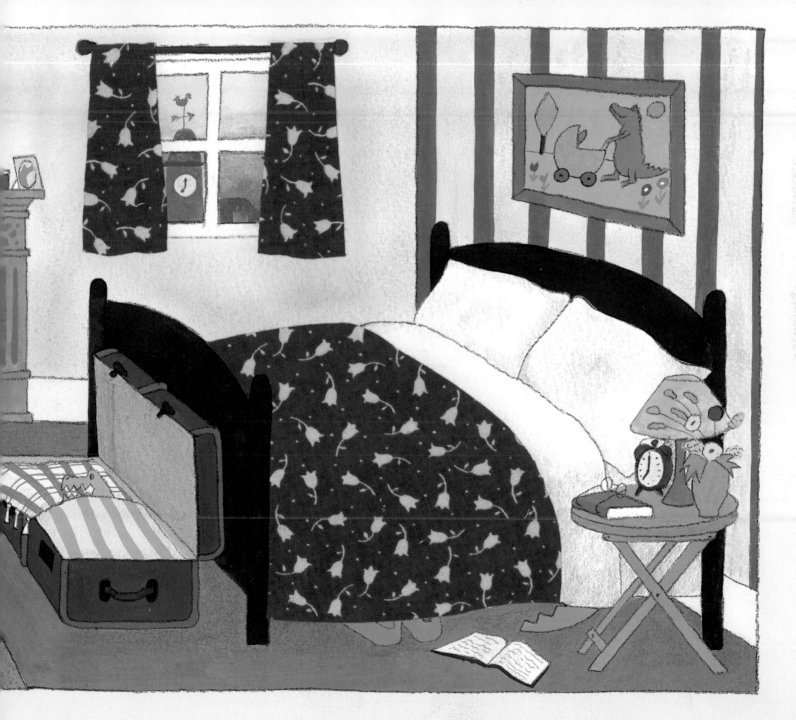

At bedtime, Little Croc hid again.

Can you spot Little Croc and all his toys?

Night, night, Little Croc. See you in the morning.

MORE WALKER PAPERBACKS
For You to Enjoy

Each book is on a different mathematical theme.
How many have you got?

WHERE IS LITTLE CROC?

Little Croc's not ready for his bath; he wants to play hide-and-seek with Mum.
He hides in lots of different rooms around the house.
Can you spot him and his toys?

0-7445-6971-0   £2.99

WHOSE HAT IS THAT?

Silly Cat has a red woolly hat; Ant has a blue hard hat. Bird, Giraffe, Snake,
Hippo and Elephant all have hats too. Can you help Silly Cat and Ant find their way
through the different mazes to meet each hatted friend?

0-7445-6973-7   £2.99

WHO GOES BUZZ?

Bee buzzes around the farm pointing out things for his friend,
Beetle, to see. But Beetle can't keep up and the scenes have changed by
the time he arrives! Can you spot the differences?

0-7445-6972-9   £2.99

WHAT GOES SNAP?

Penguin and Squeaky have lost some of their Snap cards so they decide to make
some new ones. They find things that match the pictures on the cards and, each time,
Penguin takes a photo. Can you spot the matching things?

0-7445-6974-5   £2.99